They Call Me Boober Fraggle

By Michaela Muntean
Pictures by Lisa McCue

Muppet Press
Holt, Rinehart and Winston
New York

Copyright © 1983 by Henson Associates, Inc.
Fraggle Rock, Fraggles, and Muppets are trademarks of Henson Associates, Inc.
All rights reserved, including the right to reproduce this
book or portions thereof in any form.
Published by Holt, Rinehart and Winston,
383 Madison Avenue, New York, New York 10017.

Library of Congress Cataloging in Publication Data
Muntean, Michaela.
They call me Boober Fraggle.

Summary: Unlike all the other Fraggles (furry, fuzzy creatures the size of monkeys)
living in Fraggle Rock, Boober is a natural worrier and he begins to worry even more
when he realizes that his fellow Fraggles think he is a depressing wet blanket.
[1. Fantasy] I. McCue, Lisa, ill. II. Title.
PZ7.M929Th 1983   [Fic]   83–10780

ISBN 0-03-068677-6
First Edition

Printed in the United States of America
3 5 7 9 10 8 6 4 2

ISBN 0-03-068677-6

Contents

PART ONE

Monday's Fraggle is fair of face;
Tuesday's Fraggle is full of grace.
Wednesday's Fraggle plays hard all day;
Thursday's Fraggle has much to say.
Friday's Fraggle is full of woe;
Saturday's Fraggle has far to go.
But the Fraggle that's born on Sunday
Is sure to be a great Ping-Pong player.

The Fraggle Book of Sense and Nonsense

I

Friday's Fraggle

IF you were the size of a Fraggle—which is about the size of a monkey, or a largish watermelon—you would probably be able to fit through the hole of the baseboard of the workshop of an inventor named Doc. And, having gone through that hole, you would come upon a place you've probably never been before, a place called Fraggle Rock.

Fraggle Rock is quite a remarkable place, filled with all kinds of tunnels and caves and, of course, Fraggles.

If you have never met a Fraggle, you probably don't know what, or who, Fraggles are, but I think that you would like them. The reason I think so is because Fraggles know how to have fun. I don't mean that they know how to give fun parties (although they do), or that they can play a lot of fun games (although they can). I mean that they know how to have Fun with a capital F, and they spend most of their time doing just that.

That's because Fraggles work about 30 minutes a week, and if I've figured it out right, that leaves them another $167\frac{1}{2}$ hours every week to swim, or dance, or sing, or eat, or sleep, or stand on their heads if they want to. So you see, being a Fraggle is a pretty nice thing to be. And Fraggle Rock is a pretty nice place to live.

There are always plenty of Fraggles to play with—hundreds at least—maybe even thousands! No one knows for sure, because no one has ever bothered to count them. (That's probably because Fraggles don't stay in one place long enough to be counted.) But this story isn't about thousands of Fraggles, or even hundreds of Fraggles. It is about five Fraggles who are friends—Gobo, Wembley, Red, Mokey, and Boober.

When I said that Fraggles know how to have fun, I didn't mean *all* Fraggles; I meant *most* Fraggles. Red and Mokey know how to have fun. And certainly Gobo and Wembley know how to have fun. But Boober—well, Boober is a little different.

Boober is a kind of bluish-greenish-colored Fraggle and, like all Fraggles, he has a tail. He is furry and fuzzy like them, too; but you would know Boober from all the other Fraggles because he always wears a scarf wrapped around his neck and a hat pulled down over his eyes.

The reason that Boober always wears a hat and scarf is because he is afraid of germs. Boober is afraid of a lot of other things, too. So many things, in fact, that it would take all the pages in the rest of this book to list them.

He is the first one to say, "It's hopeless," and the last one

to come out from hiding under his bed. He's weakhearted and cold-footed, and he's frequently in what you might call a "blue funk" (or in his case, a bluish-greenish funk).

Boober also worries a lot. Now, there are some things in Fraggle Rock that are *worth* worrying about. Falling rocks, for instance. And also Gorgs, who are big and nasty and not fond of Fraggles.

But Boober worries about things that would never occur to any other Fraggle—such as the end of the world, or sudden hearing loss, or not having anything to worry about at all.

2

Laundry Thoughts or Brainwashing

THE day on which this story begins was a fairly average day in Fraggle Rock. Most of the Fraggles were gathered in the Great Hall, which is the center, or what you might call the "mid-rock," of Fraggle Rock.

All tunnels lead to the Great Hall, and to get anywhere from where you are, you usually have to pass through the Great Hall. This is just fine with Fraggles, for within the Great Hall is the Fraggle pool. And if I forgot to mention it before, one of the things Fraggles like to do most is to swim. So on this fairly average day, most Fraggles were working hard at having a good time in the Fraggle pool.

Red was determined to invent a new diving stunt, and Gobo, Wembley, and Mokey were helping her make what she called a "water bouncer," which was a little bit like a

trampoline, and a little bit like a balloon, and a lot like nothing you've ever seen before.

"We could use another hand with this," said Mokey, who was holding down one side.

"Or another foot," said Wembley, who was standing on the other side of the water bouncer while Red and Gobo were trying to fill the middle section with air.

"Where's Boober?" Mokey asked. "He'll help us."

"Maybe he's doing the laundry," Wembley offered. "He sure does a nice job cleaning my shirts. He always adds just the right amount of potato starch to the collars."

"He's probably in his hole worrying about something," Red suggested. "He does a pretty good job at that, too."

"Yes," said Gobo, "but that's what makes Boober, Boober— he has his own special way of looking at things. I like that about him."

"That's true," Mokey agreed. "In fact, Boober has been my greatest inspiration for my more tragic poems."

"I don't know about that," Red said grumpily. "I think he worries *too* much. For instance, I already know what he'd say about this water bouncer. He'd probably tell me it was a dumb idea, when I know for sure that it's one of the greatest ideas I've ever had!"

"And he'd probably add that someday you could break your neck doing one of these crazy stunts," said Gobo, "which you probably could. But that's just because Boober worries about you, Red. He *cares* about you."

"I care about Boober, too," Red said, "but I still think he worries and complains too much."

The four Fraggles didn't know it, but Boober was not in

his hole, nor was he doing the laundry. He was on his way to find them. Just as he turned the corner to get to the pool, he heard his friends mention his name.

Being a naturally suspicious and insecure Fraggle, he stopped dead in his tracks and listened.

"Boober can be difficult sometimes," Mokey admitted.

"Difficult?" cried Red. "I'd say impossible!"

Gobo defended Boober once more. "He isn't impossible; he's just different."

"Difficult and different," Wembley chimed in.

"And depressing," Red added. "But it doesn't matter, because we don't need Boober at all! The water bouncer is done!"

Around the corner and out of sight, Boober leaned against the tunnel wall for support. He felt a tight little knot forming in his throat, and his friends' words echoed in his head.

"They hate me," he whimpered. "I never knew they thought I was difficult, different, *and* depressing. O anguish! O despair! I am alone and adrift—a Fraggle without a friend in the world."

Feeling miserable, Boober skulked off to find a quiet place to worry about the fact that he worried too much, and that his friends didn't like him, or need him, or even want him around anymore!

By now Red had climbed up to the highest diving ledge and was ready to try out the water bouncer. Gobo and Wembley were standing in the pool, holding the bouncer between them.

What was *supposed* to happen was that Red was to jump onto it, bounce up and over the other Fraggles, and then

LISA McCUE

gracefully dive into the center of the pool. What *did* happen was a complete surprise to everyone. With an enormous splash, Red landed in a belly flop right in the center of the bouncer, which sent the other three Fraggles tumbling underwater.

"Nice going, Red!" laughed Gobo as he resurfaced.

"Going, going, gone!" Red answered as she gave Gobo another dunk.

Mokey, who was sitting on the edge of the pool dangling her feet in the water, was writing a poem in her diary about Red's historic dive. She was trying to think of something to rhyme with *breathtaking* when Wembley swam over and tickled the bottom of her feet.

"Oh, Wembley," she giggled, giving him a good splash with her foot—just as Red and Gobo each grabbed one of Wembley's legs and pulled him underwater again.

You are probably wondering where Boober was while all this dunking and splashing and tickling was going on. Well, he was there. Actually, he was very close by—sitting in an out-of-the-way corner, right next to where a series of drips and drops of water were busily collecting themselves in a puddle.

Boober was alternately watching the puddle form and watching Red, Mokey, Gobo, and Wembley in the pool, feeling left out and very much alone.

He had always accepted the fact that he was a worrier— the way that people eventually accept the fact that they have funny ears or big feet. They simply go on with their lives, knowing there isn't anything they can do about it, and not even thinking about it very much, unless, of course, someone says to them, "Boy, do you have funny ears!" or "Gee, you sure have big feet. . . ."

That is what happened to Boober—because as he watched Red climb up the highest ledge without so much as a backward glance, and then dive from that ledge without one worried look crossing her face, it became painfully clear to Boober that his friends were right.

"No wonder they don't want me around," Boober sighed. "I'm really not any fun. I don't even know *how* to have fun— not the way Red does. She'll try anything! Crazy—maybe. Stupid—maybe. But she sure seems to have a lot of fun, and no one could ever accuse her of worrying too much."

Boober watched Gobo as he held one side of the water bouncer, and marveled at the fact that Gobo didn't look worried either. "I would have been scared to death that Red would land on my head," Boober thought, "but that probably never even occurred to Gobo, because Gobo isn't afraid of anything."

Boober glanced down at the puddle and started to worry that he might get a cold, sitting in such a damp place, but he didn't have the energy to move.

"Then there's Wembley," Boober sighed. "Wembley is so agreeable—after all, he agreed to hold the other side of that bouncing thing! Everyone likes an agreeable guy like Wembley, and why wouldn't they? It's very agreeable to be agreed with—in fact, I don't mind when Wembley agrees with me. It's when he agrees with *everyone* that it gets annoying."

Boober's thoughts drifted from Wembley to Mokey, and he sighed again. He couldn't think of anything annoying about Mokey, except maybe that she was always trying to

cheer him up. Mokey liked to help those in need, and she usually felt that Boober was a good candidate. But other than that, Mokey was a completely likable Fraggle. "I like her poems," Boober thought, "and the pictures she paints, and the nice way she has of asking how I'm *really* feeling."

Boober looked down at the puddle again, which was now slowly edging closer to the fringe of his scarf. "You and I are a lot alike," Boober said to the puddle. "No one notices if we're there or not, unless, of course, they step on us, and then what do they get? They get a wet sock, or in my case, a wet blanket."

Thinking about wet socks and wet blankets was somewhat comforting, because Boober loved laundry. Doing laundry was his job, and he enjoyed it so much that he often wished more Fraggles would wear socks and shirts so that there would be more laundry to do.

"I'll go do a load of wash, and think this thing through," Boober said. "There's got to be *something* likable about me— if I could just figure out what it is. . . ."

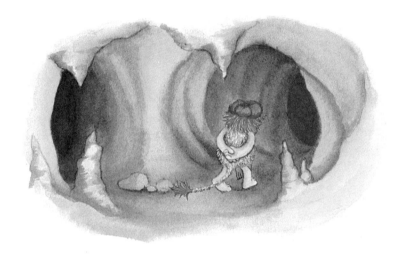

3

Being a Drag Is a Drag

BOOBER made a list with two columns. At the top of the first column, he wrote: MY GOOD POINTS. At the top of the second column, he wrote: MY BAD POINTS (According to Myself and Others).

The second column was soon full, while the first column remained glaringly, sadly, decidedly—blank.

Boober looked at the all-too-obviously-unbalanced list and sighed. Then he added a third column and titled it SELF-IMPROVEMENTS. Under the heading he wrote: Complete Personality Overhaul.

No small task, to be sure, but Boober could not forget what his friends had said. He was convinced that if he wanted them to like him, he would have to show them that he could be just as daring, just as agreeable, just as much fun and just as artistic as they were. And since he couldn't go on an adventure while watching the socks dry, the first thing he decided to do was to try to be more like Mokey. So Boober wrote the word *poems* on his SELF-IMPROVEMENTS list and sat back and tried to start thinking poetic thoughts.

He sat there a long time, regarding and disregarding a variety of topics, when at last it came to him—a poem that had been waiting, crying to be written! Boober scribbled frantically in the excitement of poetic inspiration:

ODE TO ODOR

I think that I shall never smell
A smell as great as laundry smell.
The odor of a dirty sock
For me is like a hollyhock.
Sweaty clothes, which some may think
Smell a smell they call a stink,
Know nothing of fragrant allure;
Don't know those smells can reassure.
For laundry when it needs a cleaning
Can give one's life a special meaning—
Of all the things that odors tell,
Only laundry can make that smell!

Although it wasn't like Mokey's poems about gentle breezes and happy thoughts, it was, nevertheless, a poem, so Boober tacked it up in the laundry room.

As he was gathering the clean socks, two little Fraggles who were playing hide-and-seek ran into the laundry room to find a hiding place.

LISA MCCUE

They stopped to read the poem.

"Get a load of this!" one of them laughed. "I wonder what kind of dope would write a poem about smelly laundry!"

"I don't know," the other Fraggle giggled, "but this poem sure stinks."

Boober sighed. "I should have known that my first attempt at self-improvement would be met with mass rejection." And as he turned to leave, he saw Mokey.

"Oh, Boober," she cried, "I've been looking everywhere for you! I have—"

"A poem you want to read to me?" Boober interrupted. "Sure, rub it in! Everyone likes *your* poems!"

"Boober! I . . ." Mokey began. But before she could finish,

Boober hurried off, leaving her feeling very confused, and not knowing *what* she had said to make him so upset.

But the "new" Boober was not going to give up so easily. He took out his list, crossed out the word *poems* and wrote the word *agreeable* under it.

And then, just like Wembley, Boober began agreeing with everything everyone said.

"Nice day!" someone shouted.

"Nice day," Boober muttered, although, of course, he thought it was the worst day that had ever dawned.

"Beautiful weather we're having," said someone else.

"Beautiful weather we're having," Boober said, although it could have been sleeting and hailing for all he cared.

"Have a whoopie day!" someone called.

"Whoopie day," Boober mumbled, although he had no intention of having one.

By this time Boober had made his way through the winding tunnels and had entered the Great Hall.

"I hate being so agreeable," Boober said to himself, "especially when everyone else around here is so cheerful! Before I know it, someone will start dancing and singing some stupid merry tune, and I'll have to agree with that, too!" And sure enough, someone did, and that someone happened to be Wembley.

"How do you do it?!" Boober asked Wembley.

"Well," said Wembley, "I just open my mouth, and I start singing. Then I move my feet—"

"Not *that*!" Boober cried.

"Not what?" asked Wembley, who was getting confused.

"Oh, never mind," said Boober, and he hurried off, leaving

Wembley standing there, not knowing *what* he had said to make Boober so disagreeable!

Boober continued across the Great Hall carrying his pile of clean laundry. He wanted to get to his very own hole and sort his socks, and his thoughts, in peace.

I don't know if I've told you, but Fraggles live in little rooms off the tunnels. Boober calls his room his "hole." It

is a simple little place with a bed, and lots of books, and a few things that Boober thinks bring him good luck. It is cozy enough, and comfortable enough, and just the right kind of place for Boober. He was very relieved to arrive there.

"Home sweet hole," he sighed, and slipped inside to think about what he was going to do next.

4

Brave New Boober

JUST the thought of doing some of the things that Gobo did was enough to send chills up the spine of a Fraggle like Boober. For Gobo's chosen task was to explore the many mysterious (and sometimes dangerous) tunnels and caves of Fraggle Rock. Boober couldn't imagine anything more terrifying, or more foolhardy.

"There's enough stuff going on right here to worry about," Boober would often say, "so why go looking for trouble?"

But Gobo comes from a long line of adventurers, and exploring is in his blood, or whatever it is that flows inside a Fraggle.

In fact, Gobo's uncle, Traveling Matt, has ventured beyond Fraggle Rock—beyond the hole in the baseboard of
Doc's workshop—to the land he calls "Outer Space"! (which
is actually just the real world—that is, the human world where
you and I live). And more than anything else, Gobo would
someday like to do the same thing as Matt. But first, I had
better tell you a little more about Doc, his workshop, and
his dog, whose name is Sprocket, so that you can really ap-
preciate the danger and risk that an Outer Space adventure
entails.

First of all, you should know that Doc is not a Fraggle.
Doc is a human being—a kind of grandfatherly human being
who likes to putter around in his workshop, inventing and
tinkering and building all sorts of gadgets and gizmos. (This
has little to do with Fraggles, except that sometimes Gobo
finds interesting and odd things that he gathers from the
workshop and takes back to Fraggle Rock.)

The real concern is that to an eighteen-inch-high Fraggle,
a human being looks like a frightening, towering giant. And
a human being could quite easily turn a Fraggle into a pan-
cake with simply one thump. Not that Doc would intention-
ally thump a Fraggle; he doesn't even know that Fraggles
exist. But his dog Sprocket does.

Sprocket is obviously another very real and very scary concern to any Fraggle who dares to venture through the hole
in the baseboard. You might look at Sprocket and say, "What
a great dog! Let's play fetch-the-stick!" But a Fraggle looks
at him and says, "What a great, hairy, terrifying beast! I'm
afraid he'll want to play fetch-the-Fraggle!"

Now that you understand the Fraggle point of view, I'm

sure you see that it takes a very adventurous type to set foot into the workshop, and beyond it into Outer Space—where there is a world filled with many creatures like Doc and Sprocket (and you and me).

But Gobo's Uncle Matt has done just that; he is out in Outer Space, a lone Fraggle explorer, observing and recording all the strange and wonderful things he sees. He sends his reports to Gobo in care of Doc, but because Doc does not know who Gobo Fraggle is, he promptly throws away Matt's letters and postcards. This means that Gobo has to retrieve them from Doc's wastebasket, and to do this, he, of course, has to enter the workshop. It is a very daring and courageous thing to do, and each and every Fraggle admires Gobo for his bravery.

So Boober sat in his hole, thinking how impossible it would be to act like Gobo. But then he decided that if he could do just *one* brave thing (such as retrieving one of Uncle Matt's postcards), he would never be afraid of anything again. "Everyone would like me," Boober thought, "and they would admire *me* for *my* bravery."

Boober was suddenly filled with a sense of pride and confidence. "I *can* do it!" he cried, and step by step, in his imagination, he did: He stealthily slipped through the hole and, leaping over the sleeping, four-legged beast, he ran to the wastebasket, snatched the postcard, darted past the two-legged creature, and slid toward home base. In his mind, crowds cheered and babies smiled; Boober smiled, too, filled with that strange sense of accomplishment you can get by imagining you've done something wonderful before ever actually doing it.

LISA MCCUE

With visions of cheering crowds in his head, Boober put his lucky piece of moss under his hat, his lucky socks on his feet, and set out for the hole that led to the workshop, the wastebasket, and whatever awaited him.

In the tunnel on the way to the hole, Boober ran into Red, or rather Red ran into Boober, and knocked him right off his feet. She was in a hurry to find Gobo and Wembley. She wanted them to help her with her new invention: a parachute she could attach to her feet!

"Sorry, Boober," Red apologized as she helped him up. "I've got a terrific new idea—do you want to help me?"

"Maybe later," Boober said with some enthusiasm.

"Really?!" said Red. "Gee . . . that's great! I'll see you later," and she hurried on.

"Who knows?" Boober shrugged and said to himself, "After I've proven how brave and daring I can be, I might be ready to prove how wild and crazy I can be, too!"

Meanwhile, Mokey had stopped in at Gobo and Wembley's room to find out if they had seen Boober. She was still puzzled about his strange behavior earlier that day. Gobo and Wembley were in their room, playing Fripple-Frapple, which is like checkers, hopscotch, and marbles all rolled into one game.

"Have you seen Boober today?" she asked.

"I have," said Wembley. "He asked me how to sing and dance."

"He did?" Mokey said. "That's odd."

"Well, that's what I *thought* he asked me," Wembley responded, "but I guess I gave him the wrong answer, because he got mad and hurried off."

"Hmmm," said Mokey. "He did the same thing to me. Gobo, I think something is wrong with Boober."

"That's not unusual," Gobo said very matter-of-factly.

"I mean, something worse than usual," Mokey explained.

"If it will make you feel any better, I'll go find him after we've finished this game," Gobo offered. "I'll find out what's up, or rather what's down, with Boober."

"Oh, thank you," said Mokey. "That will make me feel much better."

In the long tunnel on the way to the hole, Boober wasn't sure that trying to act like Gobo was such a good idea after all. His knees knocked, his stomach felt as if he had just swallowed a three-pound radish, and the inside of his mouth felt like a month's worth of green ceiling mold.

He was scared right down to his lucky socks, but, still buoyed by the thought of cheering crowds, he kept on going. "I'll show them all!" he cried. "I'll show them all that I'm not as difficult and different and depressing as they think!"

When he got to the hole, he peeked out very carefully. There was no sign of a beast, or a creature. But the wastebasket seemed miles away, and Boober began shaking like someone wearing a swimming suit in the middle of a snowstorm.

He was just about ready to give up and turn back when suddenly the giant four-legged beast came bounding up to the hole, his enormous mouth open like an unfriendly cave full of razor-sharp stalactites and stalagmites.

Boober took one look and fainted.

PART TWO

If you are
a poor sport,
a worrywart,
a believer in doom,
a lover of gloom,
a woe-is-me-er,
a jig-is-up-er,
an out-of-lucker,
a poor sad sucker . . .

Your name is probably Boober.

5
Down and Out

WHEN Boober Fraggle woke up, he wasn't sure where he was. He could feel that his hat was still on his head, covering his precious piece of moss; his scarf was still around his neck, and his lucky socks were still on his feet (although he was no longer sure about the "lucky" part). "I guess you can take a few things with you when you die," Boober thought. But then he heard Gobo's voice.

"Boober! Are you all right? What happened?"

Boober looked up at Gobo. "I could never explain it to you," he said, "because nothing *ever* scares you!"

And then, not daring to look behind him for fear that the

beast was still there, Boober stood up and ran down the tunnel as fast as his two Fraggle legs could carry him, leaving Gobo standing there scratching his head and not knowing *what* he had said to make Boober run off!

Boober did not stop running until he reached the safety of his hole and the even greater safety he found under his bed.

"I've failed at everything," he sighed. "I'm doomed to be a worrier—alone and friendless—for the rest of my life. I can't write poems like Mokey. I can't agree with everyone like Wembley. I can't be brave like Gobo, and now I'm too scared to even *think* about doing any of the things Red does." He took his SELF-IMPROVEMENTS list out of his pocket and tore it into tiny pieces. "What a joke," he sighed.

Gobo slowly walked back to his room. Wembley, Mokey, and Red were waiting for him.

"Did you find him?" Mokey asked.

"Yes," Gobo nodded, and he told the other three Fraggles what had happened. "I think you're right, Mokey. Something more wrong than usual is wrong with Boober."

"It's probably just one of his moods," said Red.

"Yeah, probably one of his moods," Wembley echoed.

"No," said Mokey. "I think I understand Boober's problem, and I think it is bigger than all of us."

"What do you mean, 'bigger than all of us'?" said Red. "Boober is smaller than all of us!" She was beginning to get suspicious because she could see that we-are-about-to-em-bark-on-a-great-and-glorious-mission look in Mokey's eyes.

"I mean his *problem* is bigger than all of us," Mokey said patiently, "and it will take some very clever, and dare I say *drastic* measures to snap Boober out of it. We can't just go in there and say, 'Cheer up, Boober,' or 'Let's go swimming,' or 'Let's eat turnips'!"

"Why not?" Red asked.

"Yeah, why not?" Wembley asked.

"Because Boober's problem is Boober," Mokey answered.

"But we can't do anything about *that*," Red said. "We can't turn him into someone else!"

"No," Mokey admitted, "we can't. But I suspect that's what *Boober's* been trying to do. He's been trying to be like us, and we have to let him know that we like him just the way he is."

"Then why can't we just say, 'You're a great guy, Boober, and we like you the way you are'?" Red argued.

"Because we have to *show* him," Mokey answered, "by telling him about a day when he helped each of us, just by

LISA McCUE

being there and being who he is. I'm sure we can each think of a day like that."

"But why will that make Boober feel better?" Wembley wanted to know.

"Because," Mokey explained, "he'll see that we *need* him to be just the way he is."

Gobo had not said one word throughout this discussion, but now he offered his opinion. "I think it might work," he said calmly.

A vote of confidence! Mokey was delighted, but Red was still doubtful. "Maybe we're *all* nuts," she mumbled.

6
Bad Days and Good Friends

MOKEY led the little parade to Boober's door and gently knocked. There was no answer, and she tried again.

"Go away. Leave me alone. My life is over," came Boober's muffled response.

"Boober, it's me," Mokey said. "May I come in?"

Boober didn't answer, so Mokey interpreted the silence as an invitation, and she pushed open the door. The four Fraggles squeezed into the tiny hole and sat in a semicircle facing Boober's bed. He was still underneath, curled up in a ball, not saying a word.

Mokey nudged Gobo and whispered, "Go ahead."

"Who, me?" Gobo mouthed the words. "I thought you were going to go first." But Mokey silently shook her head, and so Gobo cleared his throat and began. "Boober," he said, "I want to tell you a story."

"A fine time for fairy tales," Boober thought to himself, but he didn't say anything, and Gobo went on.

"It's a story about two friends—one who thinks he is brave and adventurous, and one who thinks he is afraid of everything. One day, the friend who thinks he is so brave insisted that they both explore a dark and dangerous-looking tunnel."

Boober began to feel uneasy; he knew the day Gobo was talking about. It was a day that Boober insisted they turn back, and he thought Gobo was still angry at him for ruining the adventure. "Why is he tormenting me by bringing this up?" Boober wondered, but Gobo continued his story.

"The brave friend ran ahead, wondering about this and that, and the other stayed close behind, watching carefully and not saying anything until he sensed that something was wrong. Then he called out, 'Stop, don't go any farther!' "

Gobo looked down and quietly added, "The brave friend was never brave enough to tell his cautious friend that that plea saved his life, because right in front of him was a deep, deep hole, as still and black as night."

"Then what happened?" Wembley asked with wide-eyed fear.

"The friend who thinks he is so brave simply agreed, and walked back, shaken, silent, and thankful that his cautious friend was with him," Gobo said.

Wembley finally realized that the two friends were Gobo and Boober, and he now understood what he was supposed

to do. "Don't feel bad," said Wembley, and he patted Gobo on the back. "I feel confused and worried and shaken up just about every single day. Sometimes I can't decide whether to turn left or right or to keep going straight, so I usually follow the Fraggle in front of me. And I'm so thankful that my bed is against the wall, because every morning I would have a terrible time deciding which side to get out on! But there was one day that was particularly awful. That was the day I stood at the fork of two tunnels for hours, trying to decide which way to go. Luckily, Boober came along, and I asked him which was the best way to go. Do you know what he said?"

"What?" Mokey asked.

"He said that both ways were terrible, so I might as well go with him and have lunch before I stood there too long

and starved to death. Boober," Wembley suddenly realized, "you saved my life!"

Red felt that this whole thing was getting a little melo-dramatic, and she knew that Boober had never once saved her life—but as she thought about it, she did remember a day he had helped her. She certainly hoped this was helping *him*, because so far he hadn't said a word.

"Boober," she said, "do you remember the day you watched me practice my backflip for the Fraggle Flip contest?"

Boober did remember, and he nodded, although no one could see him do it.

"I practiced for hours," Red explained, "and I had it down—I could do a perfect backflip. But when it was my turn to

dive, I—well—I froze. I looked down and I was um, I was"—
she gulped and took a deep breath—"I was afraid!" This was
very hard for Red to admit, but she went on. "It was terrible!
I've never been afraid in my life! But I looked at Boober, and
he knew something was wrong. He just smiled and gave me
the thumbs-up sign, and I knew then that I *could* do it. If
Boober believed I could, I *knew* I could! I guess I never thanked
you, Boober," she added quietly, kind of hanging her head.

Boober peeked out from under his bed. He wasn't quite
sure how to react, but before he had a chance to do anything,
Mokey began reading from her diary.

" 'Today I wrote two poems,' " Mokey read aloud, " 'and
I looked at them and thought, "So what?" Poetry will not
change the world. Words pieced together do not help people.
I must take action! Make a stand! Go out on a limb! *Do*

something! And I suddenly realized that I have wasted my life. What good is it to be able to paint or to write? What does it mean? Oh, Art is selfish,' " Mokey cried. " 'What torment an artist's life can be!' "

Mokey closed her diary. "The part I didn't add," she said, "is that I talked to Boober that day, and I tried to explain what I was going through. He understood immediately, and all he said was, 'Poems are poems. Worries are worries. Some people write poems, some people worry. We do what we can do, the best we can, and *that* is all we can do!'"

"Boober was right," Mokey said. "He made me see that we have to try to be the best we can be, do whatever we can do, and not worry about what other people think. . . ." Mokey hesitated. "I think I know what you were trying to do today," she said to Boober. "You were trying to be like us. I don't know why, but I do know that we *need* you to be just who you are, and that I wouldn't want you to be like me. . . ."

"Or me," said Gobo.

"Or me," Red said.

"Or me, either," Wembley agreed.

Boober crawled out from under his bed, and finally he spoke. "But I thought you'd all like me more if I wasn't worrying and fretting all the time. After all, I heard you say that I was difficult and different and depressing."

"But Boober," said Mokey, "that doesn't mean we don't *like* you!"

"Of course not," said Red. "I suppose *one* of us should be cautious."

"*Somebody* has to be cautious," added Wembley.

"And one of us needs to worry about things," Gobo said.

"*Somebody* has to worry," added Wembley again.

"You know, Boober," Gobo said, "being different can also mean being *special.*"

"That's right, Boober," said Mokey. "You're certainly one of a kind."

"I *am?!*" Boober cried. "You're right, I *am!*" And he suddenly felt better than he had ever felt in his whole Fraggle life. "You know," he said, "if any of you ever has a terrible day again, come and see me. I know all about them, and I'll be glad to help you out."

And then Gobo and Mokey and Red and Wembley, and yes, even Boober, sang a little song about how wonderful it was to be a Fraggle, and to have Fraggle friends, and to live in a place as nice as Fraggle Rock.

Boober even wrote a message (he hesitated to call it a poem) about what he had learned that day, and he tacked it on the door of his hole:

If you are like me and you worry a lot,
And you think about all of the things that you're not,
And you wish and you want to be somebody who
Isn't at all like the you that is you—

Just forget about it, it isn't worth it.

Sincerely, happily, and gloomily yours,